P9-CMS-026

This book belongs to

Perry Nash

ROBINSON CRUSOE

Adapted from the story written by
DANIEL DEFOE

Illustrated by JAY HYDE BARNUM

Prepared under the supervision of
JOSETTE FRANK
Children's Book Adviser of the Child Study Association of America

Copyright 1952 by Random House, Inc.
All rights reserved under International and Pan-American Copyright Conventions.
Library of Congress Catalog Card Number: 52-7222.
Published in New York by Random House, Inc.
and simultaneously in Toronto, Canada by Random House of Canada, Ltd.
Printed in the U.S.A.

RANDOM HOUSE · NEW YORK

WEST BEND PUBLIC LIBRARY

65-3697

FIRST ADVENTURES

ONCE, long ago, a boy named Robinson Crusoe lived in the city of York in England. His father, a well-to-do merchant, hoped that his son would follow in his footsteps and improve his fortunes. But before he was well grown the boy told his father that he would be satisfied with nothing but going to sea.

His father warned him that a sailor's life was a hard one, especially for a lad who had not been trained to sailor's work. It was dangerous, too. Ships that went on long voyages were often blown off their courses and were many months reaching home again. Sometimes, even, they were wrecked in great storms, and the men on them were never heard of again.

All this Robinson's father told him over and over again, to try to make him give up his wild idea. But the boy could think of nothing but the sea, and talked to everybody he could find who had ever gone voyaging on a ship. And then, one day, he ran away—to Hull, a seacoast town where he knew he would find ships. He had plenty of money with him, for his father was both wealthy and generous.

Now, any other boy would probably have asked to be taken on board some ship as a sailor, to earn his own way and learn to do the things that sailors have to do. For in those days, ships were not run by steam, with the big engines doing most of the work. A ship had to depend on the wind to blow against its sails and make it move across the water. Sometimes, if the wind was in the wrong direction it would send the ship toward a rocky shore, or onto sandy shallows, where it was pounded to pieces by the great waves.

Now young Crusoe had heard about such shipwrecks, but he thought, "That sort of thing will never happen to *me*. I shall sail all over the world and see many wonderful things."

And so he went on board a ship at Hull, sailing as a passenger and paying his way. He had no intention of doing the hard work that sailors have to do.

This was the first of many voyages for Robinson Crusoe. By the time he was twenty years old he had seen a good deal of the world and had had many adventures. He had been a trader; he had been captured by pirates and forced to work as a slave in their country. After two years he had escaped, in a small boat, with the help of a young African boy named Xury, and had been picked up by an English ship bound for Brazil.

Robinson Crusoe was now a fine, tall young man, strong and hardy and able to look after himself. In Brazil he decided to become a planter. He bought a big plantation, and there he raised great quantities of tobacco. In a few years he became a rich man.

Then came a time when he felt that he must go home, if only for a visit. So when he heard of a ship that was soon to start northward for England, he took passage on her, leaving his plantation in the hands of honest, capable men who would manage it for him in his absence. The business prospered, but he did not know that it would be many a long year—nearly thirty, in fact—before he would lay hands on the money his plantation earned.

And soon you shall see why. For now comes the beginning of Robinson Crusoe's really great adventure.

SHIPWRECK

THE ship on which he sailed made a safe voyage for some days along the coast of South America. Then suddenly a terrific hurricane arose. The captain steered for the nearest island, but soon realized that he and his crew must try to reach it in a small lifeboat.

But alas for the little boat—the angry seas overturned it as soon as it was lowered and the men were thrown out into the water. Battling with the great waves that surged over him, and bruised and torn by the sharp rocks in the shallows, Robinson Crusoe struggled to shore.

Presently, more dead than alive, he found himself lying on the sand. He rose and looked about him. There, a mile or two away, he saw the unlucky shipwrecked vessel, her nose poked into a sand bar, her upper parts all torn away, the furious sea still lashing at her. But of all his shipmates, Robinson Crusoe never again saw one, for he was the only man saved.

What was this land onto which he had been cast up by the sea? Was it part of South America, where he might find friendly aid? Or only a barren island inhabited by savages who would set upon him? What fate was in store for him he did not know. He was thankful just to be alive.

He was tired and hungry, and his soaked clothing was cold and uncomfortable. He walked a little distance from the shore, and to his great joy found a spring of fresh water, of which he drank eagerly, and felt refreshed.

Now it was growing dark. He feared that wild beasts might attack him during the night, and he had no weapon but the knife in his belt. Finding a bushy tree, he climbed up into it. There, held safely by its strong branches, he fell into a deep sleep.

When he woke it was a bright, sunshiny day. He could see the ship clearly now. She had floated with the tide during the night and lay on a sand bar very close to the island. The sight of her brought back his feeling of sadness at the loss of his shipmates. If they had only remained on the ship, he thought, they might all have been saved. Thoughts like this stayed with him a long time. Then he shook himself. There was nothing he could do now about what had happened. He must start making plans.

The sight of the wrecked ship gave him an idea: "Why shouldn't I try to get out to the ship," he said to himself, "and bring back what I can to make me comfortable? I may have to live on this shore for a long time before any ship comes to rescue me."

It was a pleasant enough place, this gently curving shore, the sloping hill behind it covered with trees and plants and flowers. But there were no signs of animals or men. He must be the only human being for miles around. If this were so, he would have to rely on himself to keep alive.

He walked to the beach nearest the sand bar. The tide was low now, and the sea was calm. He waded out some distance and then swam to the ship. But the deck towered high above him. How was he to scale those steep sides? After some search he found a rope hanging oversides. With this he pulled himself up onto the deck and began to prowl about. "Yes," he said to himself, "here are many things, safe and dry, that I can use. But how shall I get them to shore?"

Searching about, he found some large spars of wood. These he lashed together with rope, and after hours of painful labor, he had made a strong raft.

Now to load it. In the provision chests he found food: bread and cheese, some pieces of dried goats' flesh and a little wheat. From the store-room he took a carpenter's chest full of good tools. Next some bags of shot, a couple of guns, and a cask or two of powder—for he must shoot animals if he was to keep himself in food. Some money which he found made him smile, for he thought how worthless these gold and silver coins would be to him now. Last, but not least, he found a Book that was to prove of great comfort to him—the Bible.

Getting his heavily loaded raft safely to shore was no easy matter, and several times his cargo nearly spilled into the sea. But finally he landed his precious stores high and dry.

Next he started to explore for a good place to pitch his camp. He climbed to the top of the hill and now saw that he was on an island, with no houses or people in sight. Alone! Well, there was nothing to be gained by being sorry for himself. He must get to work to build some sort of shelter. But first, he thought, it would be wise to make another trip to the wrecked ship, for if a storm came up it might be smashed to pieces. And indeed, he went out many times in the next two weeks, each time bringing back articles useful for his camp, including the ship's dog and two cats. It was well that he did so, for one morning, after a night of storm, he looked across and saw that the ship had disappeared into the sea.

THE ISLAND

EACH day Robinson Crusoe labored long and patiently to make a shelter for himself, safe and comfortable. From some canvas he had found on the ship, he made a tent. Into this he put blankets for a bed, and boxes full of tools and food. Around the grassy spot that he had picked for his tent he built a high fence, with two rows of strong stakes driven deep into the ground. He made no door or gate to this barricade, but climbed in and out by means of a high ladder that he pulled in after him each night.

So he lived, and a whole year went by. He had set up a large post on the spot where he had come ashore, and on this he cut a notch each day, to keep a record of time. He was fast learning how to protect himself, too, and how to make the things he needed.

Often, though, when Robinson Crusoe paused in his labors, a great sadness would come over him. What if no man ever came within hailing distance of the island? What if he had to live there, alone, until he died? With these thoughts the tears would run down his face. But not for long. For then he would say to himself, "Yes, you are lonely! But those others who were thrown into the sea with you—they are gone, and you still live." And thus he would find comfort.

One day, when he was out with his gun hunting food, he found a mother goat in a simple little trap he had set, and when he had freed her he decided to take her home for the sake of the milk she would give. As he carried her over his shoulder, her baby kids trotted up, and so they went along too; and presently he had a flock of friendly, tame goats in his enclosure. Now, with a parrot he had caught, and the dog and two cats he had brought from the ship, he had a very lively family.

In all that time he saw no other human being. Yet he wasted little time in idle thoughts. And the greatest comfort to him was his Bible. He set aside a little time each day for studying it, and always felt refreshed after this reading.

At first he worried about food. What he had brought ashore from the ship would not last forever, and what would he eat when this was gone? But he caught plenty of fish and turtles and wild fowl, and in time learned which of the birds and other wild creatures on his island were good to eat. "But how strange," he thought, "to be eating game and fish whose names I don't know! And how I would enjoy a slice of bread!"

Bread! Was there any way he could get bread? He had brought wheat grains from the ship. These he could plant, and when the wheat was ripe he could grind it into flour for bread. How to grind it was a problem that would come later. First, to plant it.

But Robinson Crusoe knew nothing about farming, for he had grown up in a city. Spading the ground was easy, and he sowed his grains. But he planted at the wrong time of year, and none of his wheat came up. This was a bitter disappointment, but he had not used up all of his grains. He would try again. This time he fared better—the little shoots came up, and presently he had fine stalks of wheat in his little plantation.

By the time his wheat was ripe, he had a plan for grinding it. He hollowed out a thick section of log, leaving the bottom in, so that he had something like a big bowl. Then he shaped a thick stick into a pestle, for pounding the wheat. So, grinding and pounding the grains in this mortar, he made his flour. It took him a long time. "Not very *good* flour!" he admitted to himself. Still, it would make bread; and next time he would know how to go about the job better. For of course he saved some grains of this new wheat for next year's planting.

Then came the problem of finding something in which he could keep the flour. Many of his belongings he stored in baskets that he had taught himself to weave from grasses and reeds, but flour and certain other foods must be protected from dampness and from insects. Jars—that was what he needed—big earthenware jars with lids. But there had been none on the ship, and how was he to make any? He knew that clay was needed, and that after the jar had been molded into the right shape it must be dried in the sun or baked in a fire. It sounded simple.

He found some clayey earth, mixed it with water and shaped it as best he could in the form of a jar. This he set out in the sun to dry. But alas!—it fell to pieces when he picked it up! He tried again—and again—and again. After many experiments and failures, he finally made a strong, smooth, useful jar. Now he knew how, and he could make a whole row of others like it.

It was the same with many other things he tried to do. At first he was awkward and things would turn out wrong. But he was learning patience, and he was building up confidence in himself. Soon he began to feel that he could do anything that he needed to do.

This was a good feeling. But unfortunately it wasn't quite true, as he found out when he came to build his boat.

For he did make a boat. It was such a big boat that it took six months of very hard work to build. But when it was finished, he suddenly saw that there was no way to get it into the water. He had built it too far away from the shore, and it was so heavy that he could not pull it to the water's edge.

This was very discouraging. Why hadn't he given more thought to this, before he began to build? Why hadn't he looked ahead to this problem? Well—*that* boat would never be any use to him, except as a lesson.

He was more successful in making himself some new clothes. His old ones were badly worn, and he must have something to replace them. He stretched some animal skins in the sun to dry. Then, with twine and a big wooden needle, he sewed these into a garment of fur for himself. He even made himself a tall fur cap. And finally, for protection against heat and rain, he made an umbrella of animal skins.

It was almost a year before he started another boat. This time he built it right down at the water's edge. When it was done, after many months, he slid it into the water, and rigged up a sail. He was greatly excited with this achievement, for now at last he could take little trips to explore around this island.

CANNIBALS!

AND so five years went by, and ten more, and still Robinson Crusoe had not seen a human being on his island. Then something happened which was to bring a great change in his life.

It happened one day about noon, when he was going towards his boat. As he walked along the shore, suddenly, there before him in the sand, was a man's footprint!

He stood still, astonished almost out of his wits. Whose footprint was it? He listened, looked around him. He could hear nothing, nor did he see anybody. He wondered and worried about this for many months. But a year or two were to go by before he would find any explanation of it.

Then, one day, when he was exploring a part of the island where he had never been before, Robinson Crusoe found something that astonished him still more, and horrified him as well. It was a heap of bones, with some human skulls among them. And near by was a place where a fire had been made.

His blood ran cold, for this could only mean one thing: that at some time or other—often, perhaps—savages from the mainland came to this island, and while there killed and ate men whom they had captured. Yes, those savages must be what were called cannibals—they ate human flesh. He was thankful, now, that he had not chosen this side of the island to live on, for evidently it was here that the cannibals came. He must hope they would not come to the other side.

As soon as he got back to his camp he began to plan some way of frightening the cannibals so that they would stay away from his island. He picked out a spot high on the hill, from which he could see far out on the water, and there built himself an ambuscade—a shelter from which he could shoot without being seen. In a thicket of trees he set up a row of saplings, bound together tightly, with holes left between them through which he could put guns. He loaded several guns and braced them into these openings, ready for firing.

Every day he went up the hill to look through his screen of saplings down onto the sand. But presently he got to thinking: Why should he kill these savages who didn't know any better? They had been brought up to be cannibals. They believed that their way of life was right. Who was he to be their judge? He decided that as long as they let *him* alone, he would let *them* alone.

He felt safer, however, when he hit on a way of concealing the fires he had to make for his cooking. For he realized that savages who did come near his island would spy the smoke. One day, not far from his camp, he discovered a natural cave in the rocky hillside. Here, he decided, he would build his fire after this; and here too he would keep his stores of powder and ammunition.

Meanwhile Robinson Crusoe found company in the animals he called his family. The dog and two cats which he had brought from the ship had died of old age long ago; but the cats had left kittens to grow up after them, and by now Robinson Crusoe played with the grandchildren and great-grandchildren of his original animal friends.

Old Polly, his parrot, was still alive; and she too was good company.

And so another year or two went by.

Then, one day, Robinson Crusoe saw the first men he had laid eyes on in all these years. From his lookout on the hill he spied a fire built on the beach, and around it were a band of naked savages, dancing and waving their spears ferociously. After an hour or two they got into their boats and made off toward the mainland.

Another year passed without any other visitors. Suddenly one day he heard a gun fired. Astonished, he climbed the hill to see what it meant. There was a large vessel a few miles off, jammed on some rocks and fast being pounded to pieces. The men on board had evidently fired their gun to call for any help that might be near. Robinson Crusoe piled more wood on his fire so that the flames would rise high in the air and show the sailors that they would find somebody to take care of them if only they could swim ashore. Then he raced to the beach. But unhappily none came. Those few men who had braved the sea had failed before they reached the shore, and only their dead bodies were washed up at his feet.

Sadness filled Robinson Crusoe's heart. Oh, if only one had been saved! After more than twenty years of living by himself, he longed more than ever for human companionship. But he was not to have it—not until his last year on the island.

THE RESCUE OF FRIDAY

FOR two years more no other human being came within sight of the island where Robinson Crusoe lived his lonely life. Then, early one morning, what was his astonishment to see five canoes drawn up on the sand not more than a half-mile from his camp! Evidently their owners had landed, and were somewhere along the beach. Robinson Crusoe was both puzzled and uneasy, for there could not be fewer than twenty or thirty men in the company, and how was he to defend himself against so many?

However, he climbed to his ambuscade with his spyglass and looked around until he saw the men. There they were—savages, dancing and screaming around their fire. He was horrified with what he saw through his spyglass. Even as he watched, several of the cannibals dragged two miserable captives toward the fire. What was he to do? Was there any way that he could save these victims from the awful fate which he saw only too plainly prepared for them?

Suddenly one of the savages lifted a heavy club and knocked down one of the two captives. At that moment the other one, left standing alone, sprang away and ran swiftly along the sand—right in the direction of Robinson Crusoe!

If only he could keep up his speed, and if not too many of the savages followed him, the prisoner could find safety in the little grove of trees where Crusoe was hiding. Three men set out after him. But even if they reached the ambush, thought Crusoe, they would not be hard to deal with, for his guns were ready for them.

He did not lose a minute in catching up his gun and running down toward the creek which lay between him and the savages who were speeding toward him.

By this time, the runners were hidden from the company around the fire. Even so, when Crusoe reached the first cannibal, he did not fire his gun, for that would have made a sound that the others would hear. Instead, he hit him over the head with the stock of his gun and knocked him senseless. As he turned, he saw that the second cannibal was lifting his big bow and arrow to his shoulder, preparing to shoot.

Now there was nothing left for Robinson Crusoe to do but use his gun in the way it was meant to be used. He fired, and the second cannibal fell dead. The third, at the sound of the shot, turned and fled in terror. Now, Crusoe felt safe in looking around for the wretched prisoner who had escaped from his captors.

There he was, crouching behind a tree across the little stream. Robinson Crusoe called to him and made signs to show that there was nothing to fear. Slowly the man came forward, and timidly approached his deliverer. Then, seeing the kindly look on his face, he knelt, kissed the ground and, taking Robinson Crusoe's foot, set it upon his head. This was his way of saying that he would be Crusoe's slave forever.

How happy it made Robinson Crusoe to hear the man's voice uttering broken words that must be meant for "thank you!" For this was the first human voice he had listened to in nearly twenty-five years, and it sounded to him like the sweetest music! Here too was a companion, a helper, a friend. But he dared not dwell long on such thoughts, for he realized that behind him, stretched on the ground, was the first cannibal, only stunned, perhaps preparing to attack again.

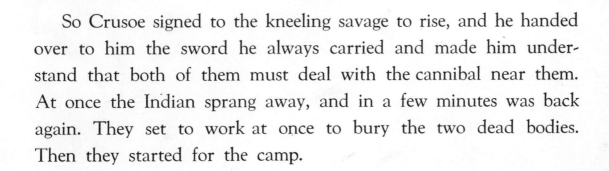

So Crusoe signed to the kneeling savage to rise, and he handed over to him the sword he always carried and made him understand that both of them must deal with the cannibal near them. At once the Indian sprang away, and in a few minutes was back again. They set to work at once to bury the two dead bodies. Then they started for the camp.

A FAITHFUL COMPANION

ROBINSON CRUSOE looked over his new friend as they walked homeward. He was a tall, handsome young fellow, with long curly dark hair, tawny skin, and sparkling black eyes. Neither of them could understand a word of the other's language, and for many days the only way they could communicate with each other was by signs. At first Robinson Crusoe kept his new friend in the cave, for fear the cannibals might discover the camp while searching for the captive who had escaped from their clutches. But when it became plain that they had all left the island, he brought him into the fenced enclosure to live.

That very first day he hit on a name for his companion—"Friday," because it was on that day of the week that the rescue had occurred. And at once there was a great deal for the two men to do, for everything had to be explained to Friday—somehow—so that he should get accustomed as quickly as possible to living the way his master lived. All the English names for things were, of course, new to him, and his tongue twisted itself almost into knots trying to shape the unfamiliar sounds. But he was such a merry fellow that both he and his master found great amusement in the lessons in English. He was quick and bright, and learned so rapidly that before long he could speak English fairly well and could understand practically everything he was told.

From him, then, Robinson Crusoe learned that some time ago, over on the mainland where Friday's people lived, seventeen white men had come ashore in distress after their ship had been wrecked, and that these men were being treated kindly. Robinson Crusoe thought that they must be Spaniards or Portuguese, and began to wonder whether there might be some way to reach them. If he could do so, they might all together find some way of traveling back to their homes in Europe. But in order to do that, he and Friday must build a much larger boat.

As soon as Friday had learned how to use his master's tools, they set to work to build a boat capable of holding twenty men.

Then one day Friday came running towards the camp, shouting that there were "one-two-three" canoes on the shore. His master climbed the hill to see, and counted twenty-one savages on the sand, and three cowering captives.

"We must go at once to the rescue, Friday," said Crusoe. Two men against twenty-one—this was certainly a daring venture. But both men were brave, and both had guns, whereas the savages had none. Besides, the attack would be a surprise, and probably many of the cannibals would take to their heels in fright.

Crusoe and his man Friday approached carefully, so as not to be noticed. Then they both fired, and immediately ran towards the group, yelling and waving their guns and knives.

Several of the savages ran to the canoes and rowed away. Others defended themselves as best they could, but the battle was over in a few moments. Then Crusoe quickly cut the ropes that

held the prisoners; there were only two now, for the third had already been killed by the savages. One of the prisoners proved to be a Spaniard and the other seemed to be an Indian.

The instant that Friday laid eyes on the Indian he gave a wild shout of joy. "My father!" he exclaimed. "It is my father!"

And indeed this was true. This old man, enfeebled and now wounded, was Friday's father. He had been captured, along with the Spaniard, by enemy savages and brought here to make a feast for them—here, on the very island where his son was living. At once Friday sped off to bring food and water for his father, while Crusoe set about helping the Spaniard toward camp. Later Friday carried his father on his back from the shore to the tent, and tended him lovingly until he grew strong again.

The Spaniard, too, regained his health and strength. After a month had gone by Crusoe told his companions that now was the time to get in touch with the Spaniards who were with Friday's people, and plan a voyage to America. So the Spaniard, with Friday's father, set off for the mainland in one of the canoes which the savages had left behind, while Crusoe and his man Friday stayed on the island and waited for them to return with word from the Spanish castaways.

ROBINSON LEAVES HIS ISLAND

FOR eight days Crusoe and Friday waited. Then on the ninth day Friday reported a boat off the southern end of the island. His master went up the hill with his spyglass, as usual. But what he saw was not the canoe he had been looking for—this was an English merchant vessel, and her longboat was putting in toward shore. How happy Robinson Crusoe felt at the hope aroused in him by the sight!—as happy as though he were a boy again rather than a middle-aged man. After twenty-seven years he would hear his own speech once more, see English faces!

But as he watched he grew suspicious. The boat drew near his shore, not far from the creek, and in it he could see some men bound in ropes. Altogether there were eleven, and three seemed to be prisoners. The bound men were dragged out of the boat as soon as it landed, and one of them in particular was evidently begging mercy of his captors. Friday exclaimed, "Oh, master! You see English man eat prisoners!" "No, Friday," answered Crusoe. "Only savages do that; but I fear they are going to kill the poor men."

He wished heartily that the Spaniard were there to help him, so that he might overpower the newcomers and rescue their victims. Perhaps, he might yet do so with his man Friday's help.

The sailors, leaving their three prisoners on the beach, started off to explore the island. This was Crusoe's chance to go down and find out from the captives what had happened. So he and Friday approached them and spoke in friendly tones. "You seem to be in great distress," Crusoe said to the man who seemed the eldest. "Can we help?"

The man, with tears of relief and gratitude running down his face, explained that he was the captain and the others were the crew of his ship. They had mutinied, seized him and the mate and a passenger, and brought them here to let them starve to death.

"Are any of the crew friendly to you, sir?" asked Crusoe.

"Yes, several of them," the captain answered. "If we could but get in touch with them, and all together overcome these others—oh, *can* you help us do this?"

Crusoe promised that he would. Friday was then sent to find out where the other men had got to, and came back reporting that they were not far away.

The five now proceeded quietly to the place where the mutineer sailors were gathered, and attacked them. A few were killed, others wounded, and the rest captured and tied up in the cave.

Meanwhile, their comrades on the ship were running up flags as signals to the first boatload of men to return to the ship. Of course they got no response. So presently they sent another boat in, with ten men, to find out what was the matter.

As Crusoe stood watching this boat approach and then land where the first was lying, he put down his spyglass and turned to the captain. "There are ten men there; they look to be desperate villains, sir!" he said.

"That means that many others are still left on my ship," replied the captain, "and of them all there are not more than three or four whom I would trust. And even with the three or four men in the cave who have promised to help us, I fear that we shall be too few to defeat the leaders of the mutiny."

Crusoe smiled. "Here are Friday and I, and you, and your mate and passenger, and two men at least up in the cave whom you think you can count on. We seven should certainly be enough for the ten now coming!"

The newcomers set off toward the hill to find their friends, calling and hallooing in every direction.

The captain suggested to Crusoe that their party should divide and wander here and there around the island, shouting as though they were the sailors who had come first and were now being looked for. In that way they might separate the men who were on the hill, by making them start out in all directions towards the shouts. This seemed an excellent plan, and they entered into it eagerly.

It wasn't long before the ship's men were rushing about, trying to find out where the shouts came from. Soon they were all
separated.

Crusoe and the captain came together at a spot on the shore just as two of the mutineers reached there. One they knocked down before he knew who they were, and the other they caught and held. He told them that he had been forced by threats to join the mutiny, and he eagerly assured the captain that he would help put it down.

By this time it was getting dark. This didn't bother Crusoe, who knew his island so well. But the darkness caused great confusion among the mutineers. At last they came together again, not far from where Crusoe and his party were watching.

"Now," said Crusoe, "here is our chance. Let us show ourselves to them, and try to parley with them. If they fire on us—but not until then—we will fire back."

"Look out for Will Atkins especially," the captain warned.

"He's the one who started the mutiny. I will point him out to you."

So, in the darkness, they crept silently to where the five men were standing. Then they jumped up with a wild shout, taking the men completely by surprise.

Will Atkins whimpered and begged for mercy, for he was a coward as well as a bully. But he and the others were tied up quickly and taken back to camp.

And now came the time for the final step in Crusoe's plan—to have some of his party go out to the ship and make the crew think it was the mutineers returning.

He would not go himself, since he and Friday would have to stay to guard the prisoners. The captain was to take the mate and all the sailors who were now friendly—about a dozen all told —and try to gain possession of the ship. By this time, it was nearly midnight, and the moon was high.

The two boats reached the vessel and the captain ordered one of the mutineers to hail her, so that the men on board would suspect nothing. Then the two boatloads of men climbed up to the deck. There was a short, hard tussle as the captain's party

fell on the sailors and overpowered them. Then the captain ordered the ship's guns fired as a signal to Crusoe that they were success-ful, and at once he put off again for the island with presents for Robinson Crusoe.

You may imagine how relieved and jubilant Robinson Crusoe was to hear those guns! To him they meant deliverance—home—England. For now he had friends, and a vessel to take him away from this island on which he had lived for twenty-eight years.

In a few days he had put his camp in order and packed everything that he wanted to take with him, including the goatskin cap he had made, his umbrella, and one of his parrots.

Crusoe and the captain decided to be merciful to the worst of the mutineers—not to hang them, as they well deserved, but to leave them on the island to take care of themselves as best they could.

And so, after a safe voyage, Robinson Crusoe saw the shores of England again. With his faithful man Friday he made his way quickly to York. Alas, both his father and his mother were dead, and all his relatives. But in time he married and had a home of his own. The agents who had charge of his estate in Brazil were very glad to hear from him, for after all these years they had a great deal of money saved up for him, so he was a rich man.

The years rolled by, and Robinson Crusoe and Friday, still companions, often talked of the island and their experiences on it. Robinson would sit by his fire and recall the terrible struggles he had gone through in the beginning, but he had to admit to himself that, taken all in all, his life there had been happy. And certainly his adventure was one of the most thrilling that any man ever had!

ROBINSON CRUSOE